FÜN學美國各學科
Preschool 閱讀課本 二版

AMERiCAN
SCHOOL
TEXTBOOK

Reading key

2

Preschool
形容詞篇

作者 ◎ Michael A. Putlack &
e-Creative Contents

譯者 ◎ 歐寶妮

Authors

Michael A. Putlack
Michael A. Putlack graduated from Tufts University in Medford, Massachusetts, USA, where he got his B.A. in History and English and his M.A. in History. He has written a number of books for children, teenagers, and adults.

e-Creative Contents
A creative group that develops English contents and products for ESL and EFL students.

FUN學美國各學科

Preschool 閱讀課本 二版

AMERICAN
SCHOOL
TEXTBOOK

Reading Key

2

Preschool
形容詞篇

WORKBOOK
練習本

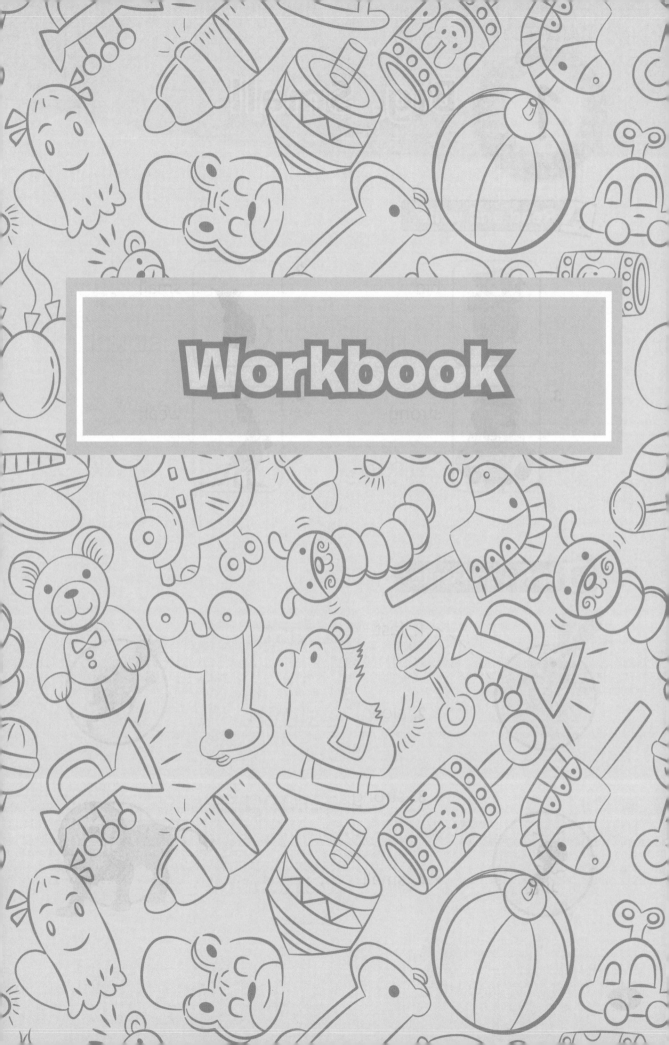

Workbook

Big, Small

 Read and write.

1.  big

big

2.  small

small

3.  strong

strong

4.  weak

weak

B Match and write.

1. fast   fast   •

2. slow   slow   •

3. strong   strong   •

4. small   small   •

1.

I am (**fast**, **slow**).   You are (**fast**, **slow**).

2.

I am (**big**, **small**).   You are (**big**, **small**).

3.

I am (**strong**, **weak**).   You are (**strong**, **weak**).

D Choose and write.

| Yes | No | am | not | slow |

1.

Are you big?
___**Yes**___, I am.

2.

Are you small?
_____, I am not.

3.

Are you fast?
No, I am _____.

4.

Are you _____?
No, I am not.

5.

Are you strong?
Yes, I _____.

2 Tall, Short

A Read and write.

1.  tall

   tall

2.  short

   short

3.  fat

   fat

4.  thin

   thin

B Match and write.

- 1. young   *young*

- 2. old   *old*

- 3. he   *he*

- 4. she   *she*

- 5. it   *it*

C Circle the correct word for each sentence.

1.

He is (**thin**, **fat**).

2.

She is (**young, old**).

3.

It is (**thin, fat**).

4.

It is (**tall, short**).

D Choose and write.

Yes   No   Is   is   not   short

1.

Is she young?
Yes, she is.

2.

Is he old?
Yes, he ____.

3.

Is she tall?
____, she is not.

4.

Is he short?
No, he is ____.

5.

____ it thin?
No, it is not.

6.

Is it _____?
Yes, it is.

3 Happy, Sad

A Read and write.

1.

happy

happy

2.

sad

sad

3.

good

good

4.

bad

bad

B Match and write.

1. we   we •

2. they   they •

3. beautiful   beautiful •

4. handsome   handsome •

5. ugly   ugly •

Circle the correct word for each sentence.

1.

I (**am**, **are**) happy.

2.

You (**are**, **is**) happy.

3.

We (**are**, **is**) happy.

4.

He (**is**, **are**) sad.

5.

She (**is**, **are**) sad.

6.

They (**are**, **is**) sad.

7.

She is (**beautiful**, **ugly**).

8.

She is (**beautiful**, **ugly**).

D **Choose and write.**

happy	sad	ugly	bad

1.

We are happy.
We are not <u>sad</u>.

2.

They are sad.
They are not _____.

3.

He is handsome.
He is not _____.

4.

She is good.
She is not _____.

DAILY TEST

4 Hot, Cold

A Read and write.

1.  hot

hot

2.  cold

cold

3.  rainy

rainy

4.  snowy

snowy

B Match and write.

1. sunny — sunny •

2. cloudy — cloudy •

3. summer — summer •

4. winter — winter •

12

C Circle the correct word for each sentence.

1.
It is (**hot**, **cold**).

2.
It is (**rainy**, **snowy**).

3.
It is (**rainy**, **snowy**).

4.
It is (**sunny**, **cloudy**).

D Choose and write.

is   was   rainy   hot   snowy   cloudy   sunny

Today	Yesterday

1. It **is** cold.   It was _____.

2. It is _____.   It was _____.

3. It is _____.   It _____ sunny.

4. It is _____.   It was rainy.

Clean, Dirty

A Read and write.

1.  clean

clean

2.  dirty

dirty

3.  wet

wet

4.  dry

dry

B Match and write.

- 1. noisy   noisy

- 2. quiet   quiet

- 3. sleepy   sleepy

- 4. hungry   hungry

Circle the correct word for each sentence.

1.

   It is (**clean, dirty**).

2.

   It is (**wet, dry**).

3.

   They are (**noisy, quiet**).

4.

   They are (**noisy, quiet**).

D **Choose and write.**

clean	hungry	quiet	dry	were

	Today	**Yesterday**	

1. I am **hungry**.   I was sleepy.

2. You are dirty.   You were _____.

3. We are _____.   We _____ noisy.

4. They are wet.   They were _____.

New, Old

A Read and write.

1.  new

new

2.  old

old

3.  car

car

4.  balloon

balloon

B Match and write.

1. cap   cap

2. flower   flower

3. apple   apple

4. banana   banana

C Circle the correct word for each sentence.

1.

   It is a (**new**, **old**) car.

2.

   It is an (**new**, **old**) car.

3.

   It is a yellow (**apple**, **banana**).

4.

   It is a blue (**balloon**, **flower**).

D Choose and write.

1. Harry has a new car.
   It is red.

2. John has a new cap.
   It is blue.

3. Tom is handsome.
   He has a blue balloon.

4. Jane is beautiful.
   She has a yellow banana.

7 Tall, Taller

A Read and write.

1. tall
   tall

   taller
   taller

2. fast
   fast

   faster
   faster

B Match and write.

• 1. shorter   shorter •

• 2. slower   slower •

• 3. younger   younger •

• 4. older   older •

• 5. cheetah   cheetah •

• 6. snail   snail •

C Circle the correct word for each sentence.

John
Tom

1. Tom is (taller, shorter) than John.
2. John is (taller, shorter) than Tom.

3. A cheetah is (faster, slower) than a rabbit.
4. A rabbit is (faster, slower) than a cheetah.

D Choose and write.

younger   faster   older   than

1.

Harry

The baby is very young.
The baby is **younger** than Harry.

2.

grandma mom

My grandma is old.
My grandma is _____ than my mom.

3.

An airplane is very fast.
An airplane is _____ than a train.

4.

A snail is slow.
A snail is slower _____ a turtle.

Fat, Fatter, Fattest

A Read and write.

1.
fat   fatter

fat   fatter

2.
thin   thinner

thin   thinner

B Match and write.

1. happier   happier

2. uglier   uglier

3. more beautiful   more beautiful

4. more handsome   more handsome

5. youngest   youngest

6. oldest   oldest

C Circle the correct word for each sentence.

1.
   John   Harry   Tom

   Tom is the (**fatter**, **fattest**).

2.
   Ann   Mary   Jane

   Jane is the (**thinner**, **thinnest**).

3.
   Tom   Harry   John

   John is the (**younger**, **youngest**).

4.
   Jane   Mary   Ann

   Ann is the (**more**, **most**) beautiful.

D Choose and write.

happiest	thinner	fattest	more	most

1.

   thin   **thinner**   thinnest

2.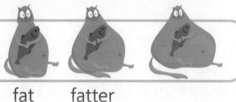

   fat   fatter   _____

3.

   happy   happier   _____

4.

   handsome ___ handsome ___ handsome

Textbook Answers and Translations

課本解答與翻譯

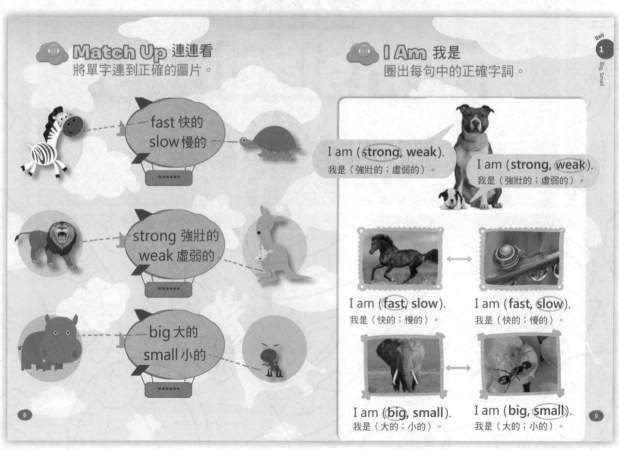

UNIT 2 Tall, Short
高的；矮的

Key Words 關鍵字彙
閱讀以下單字

- tall 高的
- short 矮的
- fat 胖的
- thin 瘦的
- young 年輕的
- old 年長的

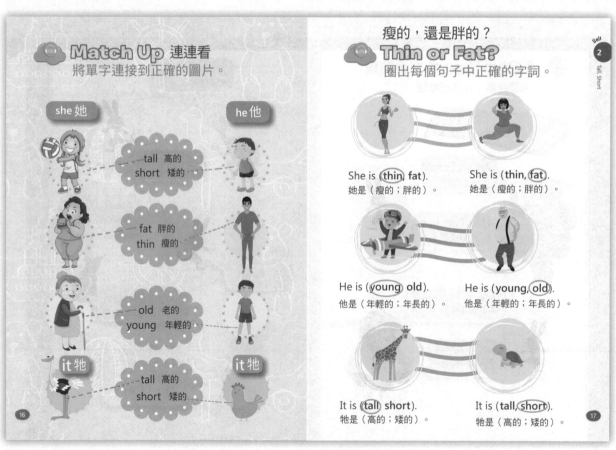

Match Up 連連看
將單字連接到正確的圖片。

she 她　　　he 他

- tall 高的 / short 矮的
- fat 胖的 / thin 瘦的
- old 老的 / young 年輕的
- tall 高的 / short 矮的

it 牠　　　it 牠

瘦的，還是胖的？
Thin or Fat?
圈出每個句子中正確的字詞。

She is (thin, fat).
她是（瘦的；胖的）。

She is (thin, fat).
她是（瘦的；胖的）。

He is (young, old).
他是（年輕的；年長的）。

He is (young, old).
他是（年輕的；年長的）。

It is (tall, short).
牠是（高的；矮的）。

It is (tall, short).
牠是（高的；矮的）。

Is She Young? 她年輕嗎？

圈出每個句子中的 Yes 或 No。

Is she young? 她年輕嗎？  Yes, she is. 是的，她年輕。	Is he old? 他年長嗎？  Yes, he is. 是的，他年長。
Is she tall? 她高嗎？  No, she is not. 不，她不高。	Is he short? 他矮嗎？  No, he is not. 不，他不矮。

Is It Fat? 牠胖嗎？

圈出每個句子中的 is 或 is not。

Is it fat? 牠胖嗎？
Yes, it is 是的，牠胖。

Is it thin? 牠瘦嗎？
No, it is not 不，牠不瘦。

Is it tall? 牠高嗎？
Yes, it is. 是的，牠高。

Is it short?
牠矮嗎？
No, it is not
不，牠不矮。

18   19

I Can Read 我會閱讀

閱讀故事，並找出朋友。

Who Is She? 她是誰？

Is she young?
Yes, she is.
她年輕嗎？
是的，她年輕。

Is she tall?
No, she is not.
她高嗎？
不，她不高。

Mary 瑪麗

Tom 湯姆

Start! 起點！

Jane 珍

Julie 茱莉

Is she fat? 她胖嗎？
No, she is not.
不，她不胖。

That's right! 沒錯！
She is Mary.
她就是瑪莉。

She is Mary!
她是瑪莉！

Finish! 終點！

20   21

Happy or Sad? 開心的或難過的？
圈出單字 not。

 我們開心嗎？
Are We Happy?
圈出單字 Yes 或 No。

We are happy. 我們很開心。
We are (not) sad. 我們不難過。

They are sad. 他們難過。
They are (not) happy. 他們不開心。

He is handsome. 他很帥。
He is (not) ugly. 他不醜。

She is good. 她很乖。
She is (not) bad. 她不壞。

Are we happy?
(Yes,) we are.
我們開心嗎？
對，我們開心。

Are they sad?
(Yes,) they are.
他們難過嗎？
對，他們難過。

Is he handsome?
(No,) he is not.
他很帥嗎？
不，他不帥。

Is she good?
(No,) she is not.
她很乖嗎？
不，她不乖。

26

27

I Can Read 我會閱讀
閱讀故事，並在正確的圖片上打勾。

You are beautiful. 你很漂亮。
You are not ugly. 你不醜。

You are good. 你很乖。
You are not bad. 你不壞。

We are happy. 我們開心。
We are not sad. 我們不難過。

They are handsome. 牠們很帥。
They are not ugly. 牠們不醜。

28

29

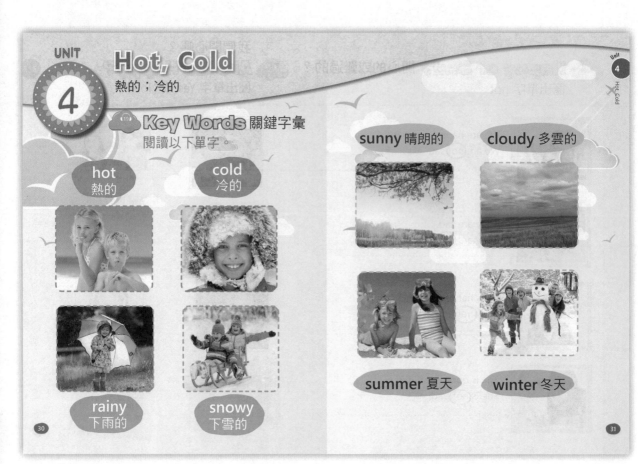

UNIT 4

Hot, Cold
熱的；冷的

Key Words 關鍵字彙
閱讀以下單字。

hot 熱的

cold 冷的

rainy 下雨的

snowy 下雪的

sunny 晴朗的

cloudy 多雲的

summer 夏天

winter 冬天

30

31

Hot or Cold? 熱的還是冷的？
圈出句子中正確的字詞。

It is (**hot**, cold).
天氣是（熱的；冷的）。

It is (hot, **cold**).
天氣是（熱的；冷的）。

It is (**rainy**, snowy).
天氣是（下雨的；下雪的）。

It is (rainy, **snowy**).
天氣是（下雨的；下雪的）。

It is (**sunny**, cloudy).
天氣是（晴朗的；多雲的）。

It is (sunny, **cloudy**).
天氣是（晴朗的；多雲的）。

Is It Hot? 天氣熱嗎？
圈出字詞中 is 和 is not。

Is it hot?
Yes, it **is**
天氣熱嗎？
是的，天氣很熱。

Is it cloudy?
Yes, it **is**.
天氣是多雲的嗎？
對，天氣是多雲的。

Is it snowy?
No, it **is not**
有下雪嗎？
不是，沒有下雪。

Is it rainy?
No, it **is not**.
有下雨嗎？
不是，沒有下雨。

32

33

It Was 過去是

在單字 is 底下畫線，並圈出單字 was。

Today 今天	Yesterday 昨天
It is cold. 今天很冷。	It was hot. 昨天很熱。
It is rainy. 今天下雨。	It was sunny. 昨天天氣晴朗。
It is snowy. 今天下雪。	It was cloudy. 昨天多雲。
It is sunny. 今天天氣晴朗。	It was rainy. 昨天下雨。

34

 It Was Not 過去不是

圈出字詞 was not。

It is cold today.
It (was not) cold yesterday.
今天很冷。
昨天不冷。

It is rainy today.
It (was not) rainy yesterday.
今天下雨。
昨天沒有下雨。

It is snowy today.
It (was not) snowy yesterday.
今天下雪。
昨天沒有下雪。

It is sunny today.
It (was not) sunny yesterday.
今天天氣晴朗。
昨天天氣不好。

35

 I Can Read 我會閱讀

閱讀故事，並圈出每個句子中正確的單字。

Today and Yesterday
今天和昨天

It is summer.
Today, it (**is**, was) hot.
Today, it (**is**, was) sunny, too.
現在是夏天。
今天天氣很熱。
今天天氣也很晴朗。

Yesterday, it (is, **was**) cloudy.
Yesterday, it (is, **was**) rainy.
Yesterday, it (is, **was**) not
　　hot or sunny.
昨天多雲。
昨天有下雨。
昨天天氣不熱也不晴朗。

It is winter.
Today, it (**is**, was) cold.
Today, it (**is**, was) snowy, too.
現在是冬天。
今天很冷。
今天也有下雪。

Yesterday, it (is, **was**) sunny.
Yesterday, it (is, **was**) not rainy.
Yesterday, it (is, **was**) not
　　cold or snowy.
昨天天氣晴朗。
昨天沒有下雨。
昨天天氣不冷也沒有下雪。

36

37

31

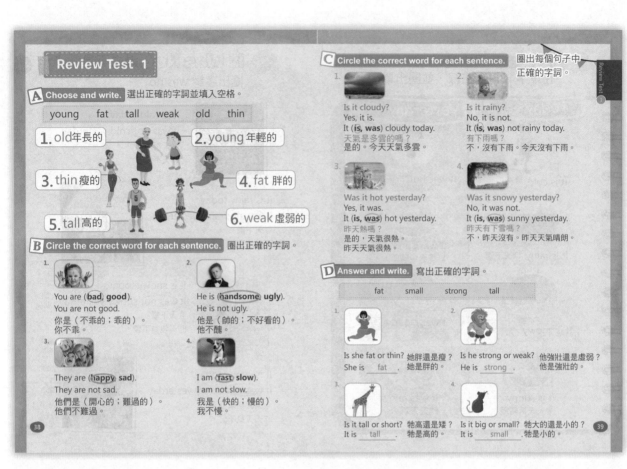

Match Up 連連看

將圖片配對到正確的句子。

It is clean.
It is dirty.
它是乾淨的。
它是髒的。

It is wet.
It is dry.
牠是濕的。
牠是乾的。

He is noisy.
He is quiet.
他很吵。
他很安靜。

She is sleepy.
She is hungry.
她很想睡。
她很餓。

42

乾淨的還是髒的？

Clean or Dirty?

圈出句子中正確的字詞。

Is it clean or dirty? 它是乾淨的，還是髒的？
It is (**clean**, **dirty**). 它是髒的。

Is it wet or dry?
It is (**wet**, **dry**).
牠是濕的，還是乾的？
牠是乾的。

Is he noisy or quiet?
He is (**noisy**, **quiet**).
他是吵鬧的，還是安靜的？
他是吵鬧的。

Are they noisy or quiet?
They are (**noisy**, **quiet**).
他們是吵鬧的，還是安靜的？
他們是安靜的。

43

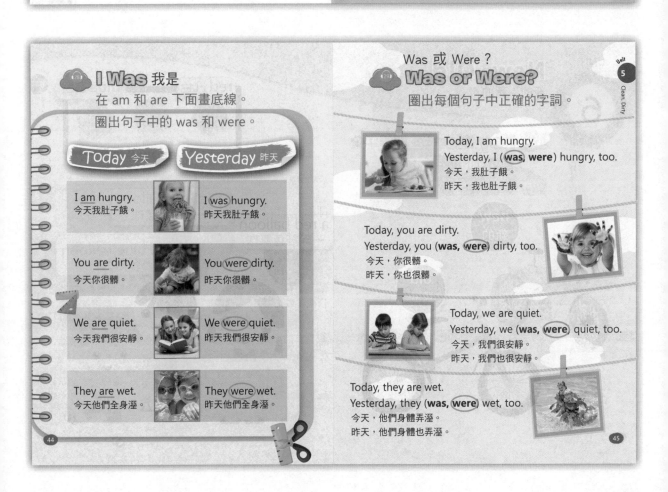

I Was 我是

在 am 和 are 下面畫底線。

圈出句子中的 was 和 were。

Today 今天		Yesterday 昨天
I am hungry. 今天我肚子餓。		I was hungry. 昨天我肚子餓。
You are dirty. 今天你很髒。		You were dirty. 昨天你很髒。
We are quiet. 今天我們很安靜。		We were quiet. 昨天我們很安靜。
They are wet. 今天他們全身溼。		They were wet. 昨天他們全身溼。

44

Was 或 Were？

Was or Were?

圈出每個句子中正確的字詞。

Today, I am hungry.
Yesterday, I (**was**, **were**) hungry, too.
今天，我肚子餓。
昨天，我也肚子餓。

Today, you are dirty.
Yesterday, you (**was**, **were**) dirty, too.
今天，你很髒。
昨天，你也很髒。

Today, we are quiet.
Yesterday, we (**was**, **were**) quiet, too.
今天，我們很安靜。
昨天，我們也很安靜。

Today, they are wet.
Yesterday, they (**was**, **were**) wet, too.
今天，他們身體弄溼。
昨天，他們身體也弄溼。

45

33

Match Up 連連看
連接字詞和圖片。

a new car
一輛新車

an old car
一輛舊車

a red flower
一朵紅花

a red apple
一顆紅蘋果

a yellow banana
一根黃香蕉

a yellow cap
一頂黃色棒球帽

a blue balloon
一顆藍色氣球

a blue cap
一頂藍色棒球帽

New or Old? 新的或舊的？
圈出每句中正確的字詞。

The car is (new, old).
這輛車是（新的；舊的）。

The cap is (new, old).
這一頂棒球帽是（新的；舊的）。

The apple is (red, yellow).
這顆蘋果是（紅的；黃的）。

The banana is (red, yellow).
這根香蕉是（紅的；黃的）。

The balloon is (blue, red).
這顆氣球是（藍的；紅的）。

50

51

A New Car 一輛新車
圈出句中正確的字詞。

It is a (new, old) car.
它是一輛（新的；舊的）車。

It is an (new, old) car.
它是一輛（新的；舊的）車。

It is a (red, yellow) flower.
它是一朵（紅的；黃的）花。

It is a (yellow, blue) banana.
它是一根（黃的；藍的）香蕉。

It is a (blue, yellow) balloon.
它是一個（藍的；黃的）氣球。

The Car Is New 這輛車是新的
圈出藍色的字詞。

The car is new.
It is a new car.
這輛車子是新的。
它是一輛新車。

The flower is red.
It is a red flower.
這朵花是紅色的。
它是一朵紅色的花。

The banana is yellow.
It is a yellow banana.
這根香蕉是黃色的。
它是一根黃色的香蕉。

The balloon is blue.
It is a blue balloon.
這顆氣球是藍色的。
它是一顆藍色的氣球

52

53

I Can Read 我會閱讀
閱讀故事，並在正確的圖片下面打勾。

Find the Friends
尋找我的朋友

This is Jane.
She is beautiful.
She has a yellow banana.

這是珍。
她很漂亮。
她有一根黃色的香蕉。

This is Tom.
He is handsome.
He has a blue balloon.

這是湯姆。
他很英俊。
他有一顆藍色的氣球。

This is Mary.   這是瑪莉。
She has a new cap.   她有一頂新棒球帽。
It is blue.   它是藍色的。

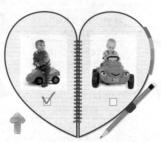

This is Harry.   這是哈利。
He has a new car.   他有一台新車。
It is red.   它是紅色的。

54

55

UNIT 7
Tall, Taller
高的；更高的

Key Words 關鍵字彙
閱讀以下字詞。

fast 快的

very fast 很快的

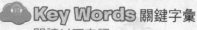

tall 高的

very tall 很高的

slow 慢的

very slow 很慢的

short 矮的

very short 很矮的

young 年輕的

very young 很年輕的

old 老的

very old 很老的

56

57

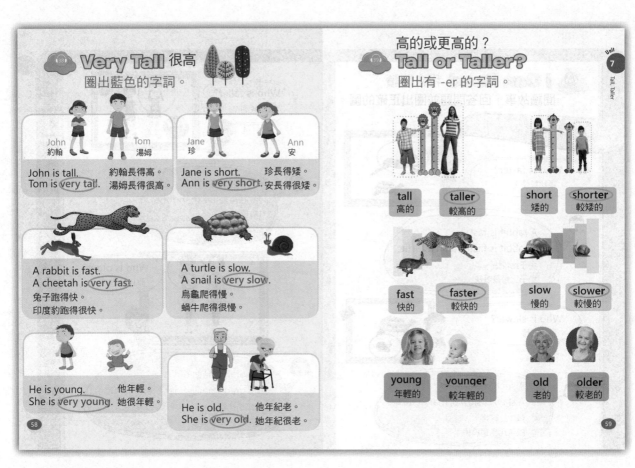

Very Tall 很高
圈出藍色的字詞。

John 約翰　Tom 湯姆
John is tall.　約翰長得高。
Tom is very tall.　湯姆長得很高。

Jane 珍　Ann 安
Jane is short.　珍長得矮。
Ann is very short.　安長得很矮。

A rabbit is fast.
A cheetah is very fast.
兔子跑得快。
印度豹跑得很快。

A turtle is slow.
A snail is very slow.
烏龜爬得慢。
蝸牛爬得很慢。

He is young.　他年輕。
She is very young.　她很年輕。

He is old.　他年紀老。
She is very old.　她年紀很老。

58

高的或更高的？ Tall or Taller?
圈出有 -er 的字詞。

tall 高的　taller 較高的　short 矮的　shorter 較矮的

fast 快的　faster 較快的　slow 慢的　slower 較慢的

young 年輕的　younger 較年輕的　old 老的　older 較老的

59

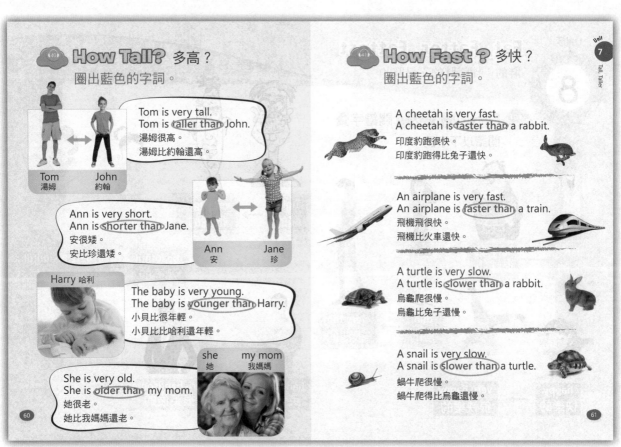

How Tall? 多高？
圈出藍色的字詞。

Tom is very tall.
Tom is taller than John.
湯姆很高。
湯姆比約翰還高。

Tom 湯姆　John 約翰

Ann is very short.
Ann is shorter than Jane.
安很矮。
安比珍還矮。

Ann 安　Jane 珍

Harry 哈利
The baby is very young.
The baby is younger than Harry.
小貝比很年輕。
小貝比比哈利還年輕。

she 她　my mom 我媽媽
She is very old.
She is older than my mom.
她很老。
她比我媽媽還老。

60

How Fast? 多快？
圈出藍色的字詞。

A cheetah is very fast.
A cheetah is faster than a rabbit.
印度豹跑很快。
印度豹跑得比兔子還快。

An airplane is very fast.
An airplane is faster than a train.
飛機飛很快。
飛機比火車還快。

A turtle is very slow.
A turtle is slower than a rabbit.
烏龜爬很慢。
烏龜比兔子還慢。

A snail is very slow.
A snail is slower than a turtle.
蝸牛爬很慢。
蝸牛爬得比烏龜還慢。

61

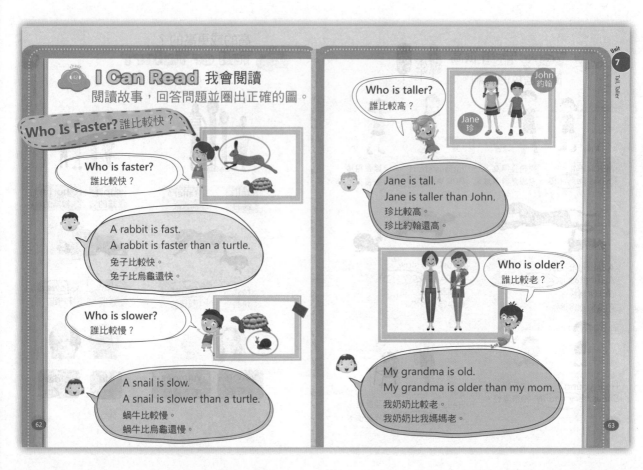

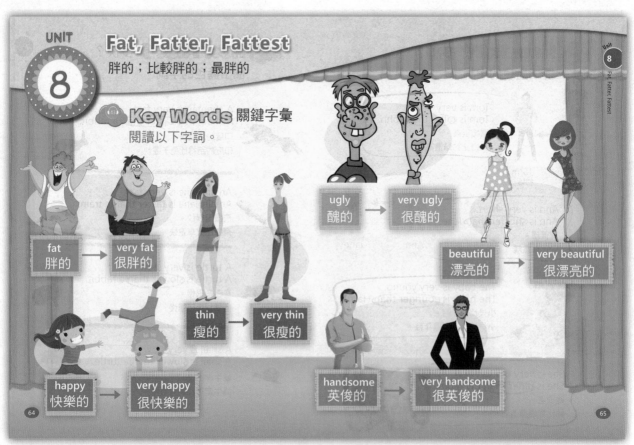

🎧 44 Fat or Fatter? 胖的或更胖的？
圈出有 -er、-ier 或 more 的單字。

fat 胖的 | **fatter** 比較胖的

thin 瘦的 | **thinner** 比較瘦的

happy 快樂的 | **happier** 比較快樂的

ugly 醜的 | **uglier** 比較醜的

beautiful 漂亮的 | **more** beautiful 比較漂亮的

handsome 英俊的 | **more** handsome 比較英俊的

🎧 45 He Is Fatter 他比較胖
圈出正確的單字。

She is fat.
He is (**thinner**, **fatter**).
她長得胖胖的。
他長得（更瘦；更胖）。

She is thin.
He is (**thinner**, **fatter**).
她瘦瘦的。
他（更瘦；更胖）。

She is happy.
He is (**happier**, **uglier**).
她開心。
他（更開心；更醜）。

She is ugly.
He is (**happier**, **uglier**).
她很醜。
他（更開心；更醜）。

Jane is beautiful.
Ann is more (**beautiful**, **ugly**).
珍很漂亮。
安更（漂亮；醜）。

Jane　　Ann

較胖的或最胖的？
🎧 46 Fatter or Fattest?
圈出有 -er、-est、more 或 most 的單字。

fat 胖的　(**fatter**) 較胖的　(**fattest**) 最胖的

thin 瘦的　(**thinner**) 較瘦的　(**thinnest**) 最瘦的

happy 快樂的　(**happier**) 較快樂的　(**happiest**) 最快樂的

beautiful 漂亮的　(**more** beautiful) 更漂亮的　(**most** beautiful) 最漂亮的

誰最……？
🎧 47 Who Is the Best?
圈出正確的圖。

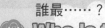

John is fat.　約翰是胖的。
Harry is fatter.　哈利更胖一些。
Tom is **the fattest**.　湯姆是最胖的。

John 約翰　Harry 哈利　Tom 湯姆

Ann is thin.　安是瘦的。
Mary is thinner.　瑪麗更瘦一些。
Jane is **the thinnest**.　珍是最瘦的。

Ann 安　Mary 瑪莉　Jane 珍

Lisa is happy.　麗莎是快樂的。
Harry is happier.　哈利更快樂。
John is **the happiest**.　約翰最快樂。

Lisa 麗莎　Harry 哈利　John 約翰

Lucy is beautiful.　露西是漂亮的。
Molly is more beautiful.　茉莉更漂亮。
Bella is **the most beautiful**.　貝拉是最漂亮的。

Lucy 露西　Molly 茉莉　Bella 貝拉

I Can Read 我會閱讀

閱讀故事,並圈出有 -er 和 -est 的字。

Meet My Family 認識我的家人

Hi!
I am Ann.
This is my family.

嗨!我是安。
這是我的家人。

I have one brother and one sister.
I am (younger) than my brother.
I am (younger) than my sister, too.
I am the (youngest) in my family.

我有一個哥哥和一個姐姐。
我比我哥哥年輕。
我也比我姐姐年輕。
我是家中最年輕的。

My dad is fat.
He is (fatter) than my mom.
He is (fatter) than my brother, too.
He is the (fattest) in my family.

我爸爸長得胖胖的。
他比我媽媽還胖。
他也比我哥哥還胖。
他是我們家最胖的。

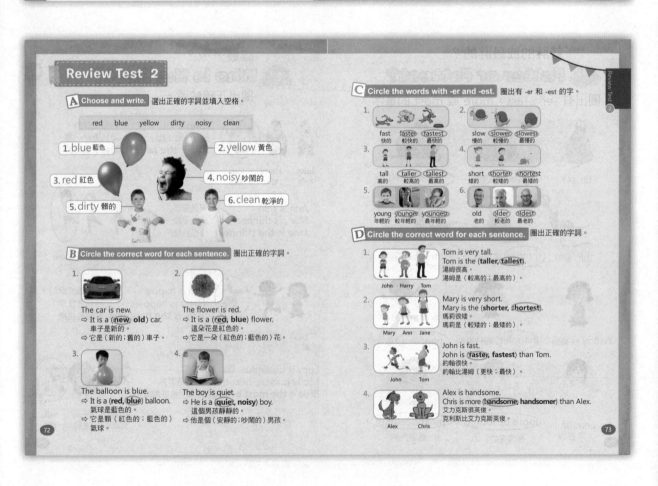

Review Test 2

A Choose and write. 選出正確的字詞並填入空格。

red   blue   yellow   dirty   noisy   clean

1. blue 藍色
2. yellow 黃色
3. red 紅色
4. noisy 吵鬧的
5. dirty 髒的
6. clean 乾淨的

B Circle the correct word for each sentence. 圈出正確的字詞。

1. The car is new.
⇒ It is a (**new**, old) car.
車子是新的。
⇒ 它是(新的;舊的)車子。

2. The flower is red.
⇒ It is a (**red**, blue) flower.
這朵花是紅色的。
⇒ 它是一朵(紅色的;藍色的)花。

3. The balloon is blue.
⇒ It is a (red, **blue**) balloon.
氣球是藍色的。
⇒ 它是顆(紅色的;藍色的)氣球。

4. The boy is quiet.
⇒ He is a (**quiet**, noisy) boy.
這個男孩是安靜的。
⇒ 他是個(安靜的;吵鬧的)男孩。

C Circle the words with -er and -est. 圈出有 -er 和 -est 的字。

1. fast (faster) (fastest)
快的 較快的 最快的

2. slow (slower) (slowest)
慢的 較慢的 最慢的

3. tall (taller) (tallest)
高的 較高的 最高的

4. short (shorter) (shortest)
矮的 較矮的 最矮的

5. young (younger) (youngest)
年輕的 較年輕的 最年輕的

6. old (older) (oldest)
老的 較老的 最老的

D Circle the correct word for each sentence. 圈出正確的字詞。

1. John Harry Tom
Tom is very tall.
Tom is the (taller, **tallest**).
湯姆很高。
湯姆是(較高的;最高的)。

2. Mary Ann Jane
Mary is very short.
Mary is the (shorter, **shortest**).
瑪莉很矮。
瑪莉是(較矮的;最矮的)。

3. John Tom
John is fast.
John is (**faster**, fastest) than Tom.
約翰很快。
約翰比湯姆(更快;最快)。

4. Alex Chris
Alex is handsome.
Chris is more (**handsome**, handsomer) than Alex.
艾力克斯很英俊。
克利斯比艾力克斯英俊。

Daily Test Answers

課堂練習解答

1 Big, Small

A Read and write.

1.  big
big

2. small
small

3. strong
strong

4. weak
weak

B Match and write.

- 1. fast **fast**
- 2. slow **slow**
- 3. strong **strong**
- 4. small **small**

C Circle the correct word for each sentence.

1.
I am (**fast**, slow).   You are (fast, **slow**).

2.
I am (big, **small**).   You are (**big**, small).

3.
I am (**strong**, weak).   You are (strong, **weak**).

D Choose and write.

Yes	No	am	not	slow

1. Are you big?
Yes, I am.

2. Are you small?
No, I am not.

3. Are you fast?
No, I am **not**.

4. Are you **slow**?
No, I am not.

5. Are you strong?
Yes, I **am**.

---

2 Tall, Short

A Read and write.

1. tall
tall

2. short
short

3. fat
fat

4. thin
thin

B Match and write.

- 1. young **young**
- 2. old **old**
- 3. he **he**
- 4. she **she**
- 5. it **it**

C Circle the correct word for each sentence.

1.
He is (**thin**, fat).

2.
She is (**young**, old).

3.
It is (thin, **fat**).

4.
It is (**tall**, short).

D Choose and write.

Yes	No	Is	is	not	short

1. Is she young?
Yes, she is.

2. Is he old?
Yes, he **is**.

3. Is she tall?
No, she is not.

4. Is he short?
No, he is **not**.

5. **Is** it thin?
No, it is not.

6. Is it **short**?
Yes, it is.

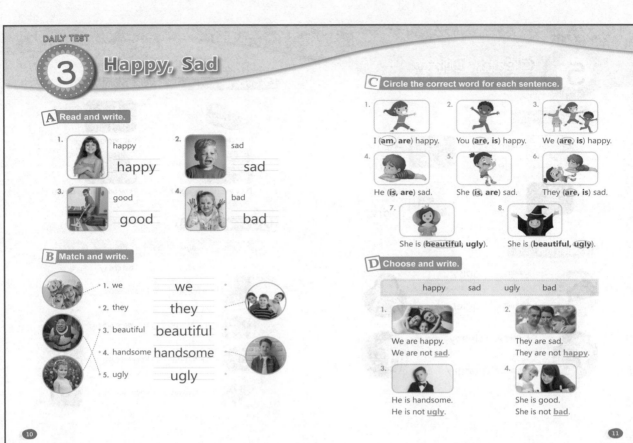

DAILY TEST

3 Happy, Sad

A Read and write.

1. happy — happy
2. sad — sad
3. good — good
4. bad — bad

B Match and write.

1. we — we
2. they — they
3. beautiful — beautiful
4. handsome — handsome
5. ugly — ugly

C Circle the correct word for each sentence.

1. I (**am**, are) happy.
2. You (**are**, is) happy.
3. We (**are**, is) happy.
4. He (**is**, are) sad.
5. She (**is**, are) sad.
6. They (**are**, is) sad.
7. She is (**beautiful**, ugly).
8. She is (beautiful, **ugly**).

D Choose and write.

| happy | sad | ugly | bad |

1. We are happy.
We are not <u>sad</u>.
2. They are sad.
They are not <u>happy</u>.
3. He is handsome.
He is not <u>ugly</u>.
4. She is good.
She is not <u>bad</u>.

10   11

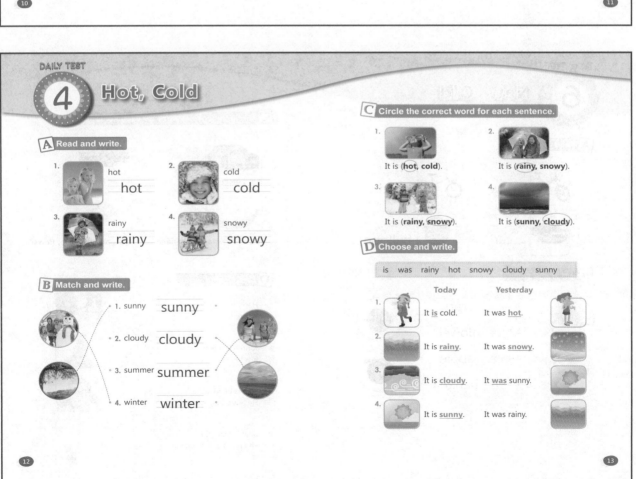

DAILY TEST

4 Hot, Cold

A Read and write.

1. hot — hot
2. cold — cold
3. rainy — rainy
4. snowy — snowy

B Match and write.

1. sunny — sunny
2. cloudy — cloudy
3. summer — summer
4. winter — winter

C Circle the correct word for each sentence.

1. It is (**hot**, cold).
2. It is (**rainy**, snowy).
3. It is (rainy, **snowy**).
4. It is (sunny, **cloudy**).

D Choose and write.

| is | was | rainy | hot | snowy | cloudy | sunny |

	Today	Yesterday	
1.	It <u>is</u> cold.	It was <u>hot</u>.	
2.	It is <u>rainy</u>.	It was <u>snowy</u>.	
3.	It is <u>cloudy</u>.	It <u>was</u> sunny.	
4.	It is <u>sunny</u>.	It was rainy.	

12   13

5 Clean, Dirty

A Read and write.

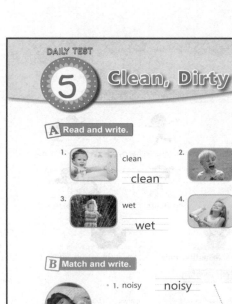

1. clean — **clean**
2. dirty — **dirty**
3. wet — **wet**
4. dry — **dry**

B Match and write.

1. noisy — **noisy**
2. quiet — **quiet**
3. sleepy — **sleepy**
4. hungry — **hungry**

C Circle the correct word for each sentence.

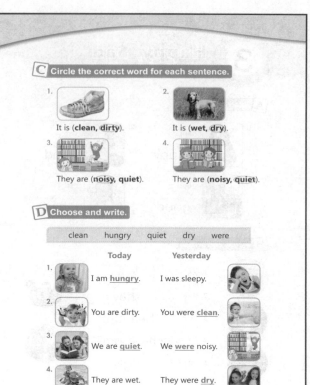

1. It is (**clean, dirty**).
2. It is (**wet, dry**).
3. They are (**noisy, quiet**).
4. They are (noisy, **quiet**).

D Choose and write.

| clean | hungry | quiet | dry | were |

	Today	Yesterday	
1.	I am <u>hungry</u>.	I was sleepy.	
2.	You are dirty.	You were <u>clean</u>.	
3.	We are <u>quiet</u>.	We <u>were</u> noisy.	
4.	They are wet.	They were <u>dry</u>.	

14

15

---

6 New, Old

A Read and write.

1. new — **new**
2. old — **old**
3. car — **car**
4. balloon — **balloon**

B Match and write.

1. cap — **cap**
2. flower — **flower**
3. apple — **apple**
4. banana — **banana**

C Circle the correct word for each sentence.

1. It is a (**new, old**) car.
2. It is an (new, **old**) car.
3. It is a yellow (apple, **banana**).
4. It is a blue (**balloon**, flower).

D Choose and write.

1. Harry has a new car.
   It is red.

2. John has a new cap.
   It is blue.

3. Tom is handsome.
   He has a blue balloon.

4. Jane is beautiful.
   She has a yellow banana.

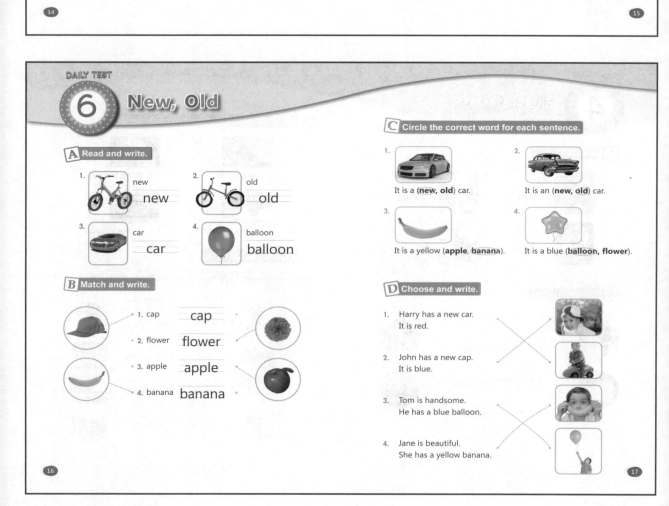

16

17

DAILY TEST 7 — Tall, Taller

A Read and write.

1. tall

tall — taller **taller**

2. fast

fast — faster **faster**

B Match and write.

1. shorter **shorter**
2. slower **slower**
3. younger **younger**
4. older **older**
5. cheetah **cheetah**
6. snail **snail**

C Circle the correct word for each sentence.

1. Tom is (**taller**, shorter) than John.
2. John is (taller, **shorter**) than Tom.

3. A cheetah is (**faster**, slower) than a rabbit.
4. A rabbit is (faster, **slower**) than a cheetah.

D Choose and write.

younger	faster	older	than

1.
The baby is very young.
The baby is **younger** than Harry.

2.
My grandma is old.
My grandma is **older** than my mom.

3.
An airplane is very fast.
An airplane is **faster** than a train.

4.
A snail is slow.
A snail is slower **than** a turtle.

18   19

DAILY TEST 8 — Fat, Fatter, Fattest

A Read and write.

1. fat

fat — fatter **fatter**

2. thin

thin — thinner **thinner**

B Match and write.

1. happier **happier**
2. uglier **uglier**
3. more beautiful **more beautiful**
4. more handsome **more handsome**
5. youngest **youngest**
6. oldest **oldest**

C Circle the correct word for each sentence.

1. Tom is the (fatter, **fattest**).
John Harry Tom

2. Jane is the (thinner, **thinnest**).
Ann Mary Jane

3. John is the (younger, **youngest**).
Tom Harry John

4. Ann is the (more, **most**) beautiful.
Jane Mary Ann

D Choose and write.

happiest	thinner	fattest	more	most

1.
thin **thinner** thinnest

2.
fat fatter **fattest**

3. happy happier **happiest**

4. handsome **more** handsome **most** handsome

20   21

45

weak

strong

fast

slow

Match Up

Match the words with the pictures.

fast

slow

strong

weak

big

small

I Am

Circle the correct word for each sentence.

I am (**strong**, weak).

I am (**strong**, weak).

I am (**fast**, slow).

I am (fast, **slow**).

I am (**big**, small).

I am (big, **small**).

You Are

Circle the correct word for each sentence.

You are (**strong, weak**).

You are (**strong, weak**).

You are (**fast, slow**).

You are (**fast, slow**).

You are (**big, small**).

You are (**big, small**).

Are You Big?

Circle the word **Yes** or **No**.

I Can Read Read the story. Find the animal.

Who Am I?

Are you big?

No, I am not.

Are you strong?

No, I am not.

UNIT 2

Tall, Short

🎧 07 Key Words

Read the words.

tall

short

14

fat

thin

young

old

Match Up

Match the words with the pictures.

she

tall

short

he

fat

thin

old

young

it

tall

short

it

Thin or Fat?

Circle the correct word for each sentence.

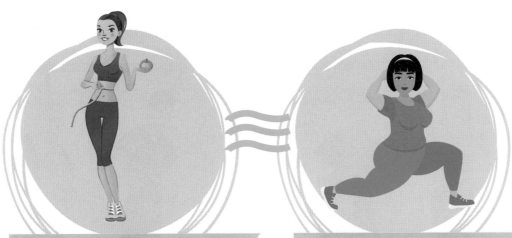

She is (**thin**, **fat**).   She is (**thin**, **fat**).

He is (**young**, **old**).   He is (**young**, **old**).

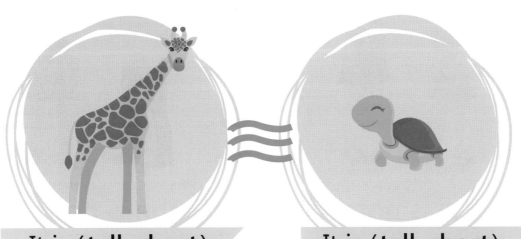

It is (**tall**, **short**).   It is (**tall**, **short**).

Is She Young?

Circle the word **Yes** or **No**.

Is she young?

Yes, she is.

Is he old?

Yes, he is.

Is she tall?

No, she is not.

Is he short?

No, he is not.

 **Is It Fat?**

(Circle) the words **is** and **is not**.

Is it fat?
Yes, it is.

Is it thin?
No, it is not.

Is it tall?
Yes, it is.

Is it short?
No, it is not.

I Can Read Read the story. Find the friend.

Who Is She?

?

Is she young?
Yes, she is.

Mary

Start!

Tom

Jane

Julie

Is she tall?
No, she is not.

Is she fat?
No, she is not.

She is Mary!

That's right!
She is Mary.

Finish!

UNIT 3 Happy, Sad

🎧13 Key Words Read the words.

happy

sad

good

bad

beautiful

ugly

handsome

Match Up

Match the words with the pictures.

happy

sad

good

bad

beautiful

ugly

handsome

I Am Happy

Circle the words **in blue**.

I am happy.   You are happy.   We are happy.

He is sad.   She is sad.   They are sad.

She is beautiful.   She is ugly.

Happy or Sad?

Circle the word **not**.

We are happy.
We are (not) sad.

They are sad.
They are not happy.

He is handsome.
He is not ugly.

She is good.
She is not bad.

Are We Happy?

Circle the word **Yes** or **No**.

Are we happy?
Yes, we are.

Are they sad?
Yes, they are.

Is he handsome?
No, he is not.

Is she good?
No, she is not.

I Can Read

Read the story. Put a check under the correct picture.

You are beautiful.
You are not ugly.

You are good.
You are not bad.

We are happy.
We are not sad.

They are handsome.
They are not ugly.

4

Hot, Cold

 Key Words Read the words.

hot

cold

rainy

snowy

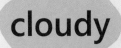
sunny

cloudy

summer

winter

Hot or Cold?

Circle the correct word for each sentence.

It is (**hot**, cold).

It is (hot, **cold**).

It is (**rainy**, snowy).

It is (rainy, **snowy**).

It is (**sunny**, cloudy).

It is (sunny, **cloudy**).

Is It Hot?

21

(Circle) the words **is** and **is not**.

Is it hot?
Yes, it is.

Is it cloudy?
Yes, it is.

Is it snowy?
No, it is not.

Is it rainy?
No, it is not.

It Was

Underline the word **is**. Circle the word **was**.

It <u>is</u> cold.

It (was) hot.

It is rainy.

It was sunny.

It is snowy.

It was cloudy.

It is sunny.

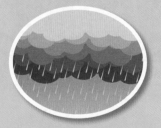

It was rainy.

It Was Not

Circle the words **was not**.

It is cold today.
It (was not) cold yesterday.

It is rainy today.
It was not rainy yesterday.

It is snowy today.
It was not snowy yesterday.

It is sunny today.
It was not sunny yesterday.

I Can Read

Read the story. (Circle) the correct word for each sentence.

Today and Yesterday

It is summer.
Today, it (**is**, **was**) hot.
Today, it (**is**, **was**)
sunny, too.

Yesterday, it (**is**, **was**) cloudy.
Yesterday, it (**is**, **was**) rainy.
Yesterday, it (**is**, **was**) not
hot or sunny.

It is winter.
Today, it (**is, was**) cold.
Today, it (**is, was**) snowy, too.

Yesterday, it (**is, was**) sunny.
Yesterday, it (**is, was**) not rainy.
Yesterday, it (**is, was**) not
    cold or snowy.

A Choose and write.

young   fat   tall   weak   old   thin

1. old

2.

3.

4.

5.

6.

B Circle the correct word for each sentence.

1.

You are (**bad, good**).
You are not good.

2.

He is (**handsome, ugly**).
He is not ugly.

3.

They are (**happy, sad**).
They are not sad.

4.

I am (**fast, slow**).
I am not slow.

C Circle the correct word for each sentence.

1.

Is it cloudy?
Yes, it is.
It (**is**, **was**) cloudy today.

2.

Is it rainy?
No, it is not.
It (**is**, **was**) not rainy today.

3.

Was it hot yesterday?
Yes, it was.
It (**is**, **was**) hot yesterday.

4.

Was it snowy yesterday?
No, it was not.
It (**is**, **was**) sunny yesterday.

D Answer and write.

fat   small   strong   tall

1.

Is she fat or thin?
She is ___fat___.

2.

Is he strong or weak?
He is _____.

3.

Is it tall or short?
It is _____.

4.

Is it big or small?
It is _____.

39

5 Clean, Dirty

 **Key Words** Read the words.

clean

dirty

wet

dry

noisy

quiet

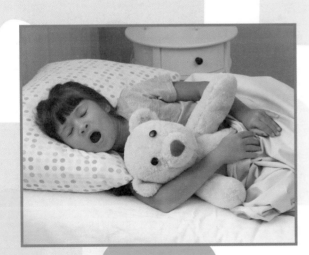

sleepy

hungry

 **Match Up**

Match each picture with the correct sentence.

- It is clean.
- It is dirty.

- It is wet.
- It is dry.

- He is noisy.
- He is quiet.

- She is sleepy.
- She is hungry.

Clean or Dirty?

Circle the correct word for each sentence.

Is it clean or dirty?
It is (**clean**, (**dirty**)).

Is it wet or dry?
It is (**wet, dry**).

Is he noisy or quiet?
He is (**noisy, quiet**).

Are they noisy or quiet?
They are (**noisy, quiet**).

 **I Was** Underline the words **am** and **are**.

Circle the words **was** and **were**.

 Today

 Yesterday

I am hungry.

I was hungry.

You are dirty.

You were dirty.

We are quiet.

We were quiet.

They are wet.

They were wet.

Was or Were?

(Circle) the correct word for each sentence.

Today, I am hungry.

Yesterday, I (**was**, **were**) hungry, too.

Today, you are dirty.

Yesterday, you (**was**, **were**) dirty, too.

Today, we are quiet.

Yesterday, we (**was**, **were**) quiet, too.

Today, they are wet.

Yesterday, they (**was**, **were**) wet, too.

I Can Read

Read the story. Circle the correct word for each sentence.

Today and Yesterday

Today, I am dirty.

Yesterday, I was not dirty.
I was (**clean**, **dirty**).

Today, you are clean.

Yesterday, you were not clean.
You were (**clean, dirty**).

Today, we are quiet.

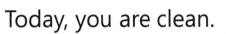

Yesterday, we were not quiet.
We were (**noisy, quiet**).

UNIT 6
New, Old

Key Words

Read the words.

new

old

48

Match Up

Match the words with the pictures.

a new car

an old car

a red flower

a red apple

a yellow banana

a yellow cap

a blue balloon

a blue cap

New or Old?

Circle the correct word for each sentence.

The car is (**new**, **old**).

The cap is (**new**, **old**).

The apple is (**red**, **yellow**).

The banana is (**red**, **yellow**).

The balloon is (**blue**, **red**).

 # A New Car

Circle the correct word for each sentence.

It is a (**new**, **old**) car.

It is an (**new**, **old**) car.

It is a (**red**, **yellow**) flower.

It is a (**yellow**, **blue**) banana.

It is a (**blue**, **yellow**) balloon.

The Car Is New

(35)

Circle the words **in blue**.

The car is (new).
It is a (new) car.

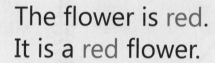
The flower is red.
It is a red flower.

The banana is yellow.
It is a yellow banana.

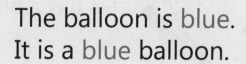
The balloon is blue.
It is a blue balloon.

I Can Read

Read the story. Put a check under the correct picture.

Find the Friends

This is Jane.
She is beautiful.
She has a yellow banana.

This is Tom.
He is handsome.
He has a blue balloon.

This is Mary.
She has a new cap.
It is blue.

This is Harry.
He has a new car.
It is red.

Tall, Taller

 Key Words Read the words.

tall

very tall

short

very short

fast

very fast

slow

very slow

young

very young

old

very old

Very Tall

Circle the words **in blue**.

John is tall.
Tom is (very tall.)

Jane is short.
Ann is **very short**.

A rabbit is fast.
A cheetah is **very fast**.

A turtle is slow.
A snail is **very slow**.

He is young.
She is **very young**.

He is old.
She is **very old**.

Tall or Taller?

39

Circle the words with **-er**.

tall　　　　**taller**

short　　　　**shorter**

fast　　　　**faster**

slow　　　　**slower**

young　　　**younger**

old　　　　**older**

How Tall?

Circle the words **in blue**.

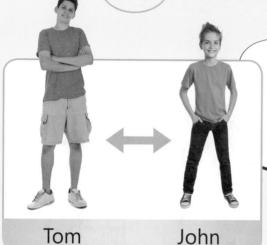

Tom

John

Tom is very tall.
Tom is ⟨**taller than**⟩ John.

Ann

Jane

Ann is very short.
Ann is **shorter than** Jane.

Harry

The baby is very young.
The baby is **younger than** Harry.

she

my mom

She is very old.
She is **older than** my mom.

How Fast ?

Circle the words **in blue**

A cheetah is very fast.

A cheetah is (faster than) a rabbit.

An airplane is very fast.

An airplane is **faster than** a train.

A turtle is very slow.

A turtle is **slower than** a rabbit.

A snail is very slow.

A snail is **slower than** a turtle.

I Can Read Read the story.

Answer the questions. Circle the correct pictures.

Who Is Faster?

Who is faster?

A rabbit is fast.
A rabbit is faster than a turtle.

Who is slower?

A snail is slow.
A snail is slower than a turtle.

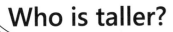

Who is taller?

Jane

John

Jane is tall.
Jane is taller than John.

Who is older?

My grandma is old.
My grandma is older than my mom.

Fat, Fatter, Fattest

43 **Key Words** Read the words.

fat → very fat

thin → very thin

happy → very happy

ugly ⟶ very ugly

beautiful ⟶ very beautiful

handsome ⟶ very handsome

Fat or Fatter?

(Circle) the words with **-er** and **-ier** and **more**.

fat   (fatt**er**)

thin   thinn**er**

happy   happ**ier**

ugly   ugl**ier**

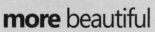

beautiful   **more** beautiful

handsome   **more** handsome

He Is Fatter

Circle the correct word for each sentence.

She is fat.
He is (**thinner**, **fatter**).

She is thin.
He is (**thinner**, **fatter**).

She is happy.
He is (**happier**, **uglier**).

She is ugly.
He is (**happier**, **uglier**).

Jane   Ann

Jane is beautiful.
Ann is more (**beautiful**, **ugly**).

Fatter or Fattest?

Circle the words with **-er** and **-est**, **more**, and **most**.

fat   fatter   fattest

thin   thinner   thinnest

happy   happier   happiest

beautiful   **more** beautiful   **most** beautiful

Who Is the Best?

(Circle) the correct pictures.

John   Harry   Tom

John is fat.
Harry is fatter.
Tom is **the fattest**.

Ann is thin.
Mary is thinner.
Jane is **the thinnest**.

Ann   Mary   Jane

Lisa   Harry   John

Lisa is happy.
Harry is happier.
John is **the happiest**.

Lucy is beautiful.
Molly is more beautiful.
Bella is **the most beautiful**.

Lucy   Molly   Bella

I Can Read

Read the story. Circle the words with **-er** and **-est**.

Meet My Family

Hi!
I am Ann.
This is my family.

I have one brother and one sister.
I am younger than my brother.
I am younger than my sister, too.
I am the youngest in my family.

My dad is fat.

He is fatter than my mom.

He is fatter than my brother, too.

He is the fattest in my family.

Review Test 2

A Choose and write.

red   blue   yellow   dirty   noisy   clean

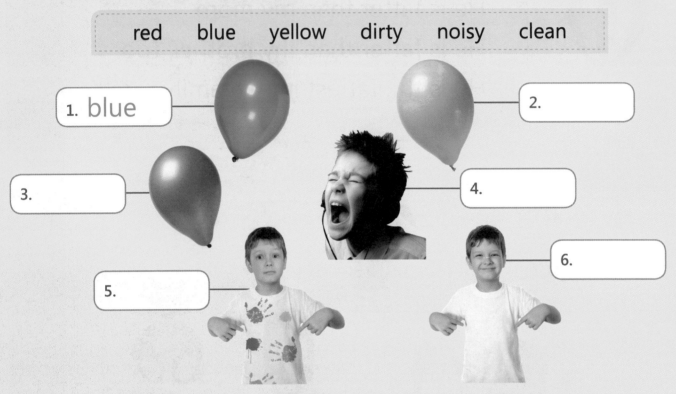

1. blue

2.

3.

4.

5.

6.

B Circle the correct word for each sentence.

1.

The car is new.
⇨ It is a (**new**, **old**) car.

2.

The flower is red.
⇨ It is a (**red**, **blue**) flower.

3.

The balloon is blue.
⇨ It is a (**red**, **blue**) balloon.

4.

The boy is quiet.
⇨ He is a (**quiet**, **noisy**) boy.

72

C Circle the words with -er and -est.

1.

fast (faster) (fastest)

2.

slow slower slowest

3.

tall taller tallest

4.

short shorter shortest

5.

young younger youngest

6.

old older oldest

D Circle the correct word for each sentence.

1.

John Harry Tom

Tom is very tall.
Tom is the (**taller,** (**tallest**)).

2.

Mary Ann Jane

Mary is very short.
Mary is the (**shorter, shortest**).

3.

John Tom

John is fast.
John is (**faster, fastest**) than Tom.

4.

Alex Chris

Alex is handsome.
Chris is more (**handsome, handsomer**) than Alex.

Word List

Big, Small
大的，小的

1. **big** 大的
2. **small** 小的
3. **strong** 強壯的
4. **weak** 虛弱的
5. **fast** 快的
6. **slow** 慢的
7. **I am . . .** 我是……
8. **You are . . .** 你是……
9. **Are you big?** 你很大嗎？
10. **Yes, I am.** 對，我很大。
11. **No, I am not.** 不，我不大。
12. **Who am I?** 我是誰？
13. **rabbit** 兔子
14. **That's right.** 沒錯。

Tall, Short
高的，矮的

1. **tall** 高的
2. **short** 矮的
3. **fat** 胖的
4. **thin** 瘦的
5. **young** 年輕的
6. **old** 老的
7. **she** 她
8. **he** 他
9. **it** 牠
10. **She is . . .** 她是……
11. **He is . . .** 他是……
12. **It is . . .** 牠是……
13. **Is she young?** 她年輕嗎？
14. **Yes, she is.** 對，她很年輕。
15. **No, she is not.** 不，她不年輕。
16. **Is it fat?** 牠胖嗎？
17. **Yes, it is.** 對，牠很胖。

18	**No, it is not.**	不，牠不胖。	
19	**find**	找到	
20	**friend**	朋友	
21	**Find the friend.**	找到那個朋友。	

Unit 3

Happy, Sad
開心的，難過的

1	**happy**	開心的
2	**sad**	難過的
3	**good**	好的
4	**bad**	壞的
5	**beautiful**	美麗的
6	**ugly**	醜陋的
7	**handsome**	帥氣的
8	**We are . . .**	我們是……
9	**They are . . .**	他們是……
10	**We are not . . .**	我們不是……
11	**Are we happy?**	我們開心嗎？
12	**Yes, we are.**	對，我們很開心。
13	**Are they sad?**	他們難過嗎？
14	**Yes, they are.**	對，他們很難過。
15	**Is he handsome?**	他帥氣嗎？
16	**No, he is not.**	不，他不帥。

Unit 4

Hot, Cold
熱的，冷的

1	**hot**	熱的
2	**cold**	冷的
3	**rainy**	下雨的
4	**snowy**	下雪的
5	**sunny**	天氣晴朗的
6	**cloudy**	多雲的
7	**summer**	夏天
8	**winter**	冬天
9	**It is . . .**	天氣是……
10	**It is hot.**	天氣是熱的。
11	**Is it hot?**	天氣是熱的嗎？
12	**Yes, it is.**	對，天氣是熱的。
13	**No, it is not.**	不，天氣不熱。
14	**today**	今天
15	**yesterday**	昨天
16	**It was . . .**	天氣之前是……
17	**It was not . . .**	天氣之前不是……
18	**too**	也

Unit 5

Clean, Dirty
乾淨的，髒亂的

1	clean	乾淨的
2	dirty	髒亂的
3	wet	濕的
4	dry	乾的
5	noisy	吵鬧的
6	quiet	安靜的
7	sleepy	想睡的
8	hungry	飢餓的
9	or	或者
10	Is it clean or dirty? 它是乾淨的，還是髒的？	
11	I was . . .	我以前是……
12	You were . . .	你以前是……
13	We were . . .	我們以前是……
14	They were . . .	他們以前是……

Unit 6

New, Old
新的，舊的

1	new	新的
2	old	舊的
3	red	紅色；紅色的
4	yellow	黃色；黃色的

5	blue	藍色；藍色的
6	a red balloon	一顆紅色的氣球
7	a yellow balloon	一顆黃色的氣球
8	a blue balloon	一顆藍色的氣球
9	a new car	一輛新車
10	an old car	一輛舊車
11	a red flower	一朵紅色的花
12	a red apple	一顆紅色的蘋果
13	a yellow banana	一根黃色的香蕉
14	a yellow cap	一頂黃色的帽子
15	a blue cap	一頂藍色的帽子
16	This is . . .	這是……
17	has	有

Unit 7

Tall, Taller
高的，較高的

1	very	非常；很
2	very tall	非常高
3	very short	非常矮
4	very fast	非常快
5	very slow	非常慢
6	very young	非常年輕
7	very old	非常老
8	rabbit	兔子
9	cheetah	獵豹；印度豹
10	turtle	烏龜

11	snail	蝸牛
12	taller	較高的
13	shorter	較矮的
14	faster	較快的
15	slower	較慢的
16	younger	較年輕的
17	older	較老的
18	How tall?	多高？
19	be taller than	比……高
20	be shorter than	比……矮
21	be younger than	比……年輕
22	be older than	比……老
23	mom	媽媽；母親
24	How fast?	多快？
25	be faster than	比……快
26	airplane	飛機
27	train	火車
28	be slower than	比……慢
29	Who is faster?	誰比較快？
30	Who is slower?	誰比較慢？
31	Who is taller?	誰比較高？
32	Who is older?	誰比較老？
33	grandma	奶奶；外婆

Unit 8

Fat, Fatter, Fattest
胖的，較胖的，最胖的

1	very fat	非常胖
2	very thin	非常瘦
3	very happy	非常開心
4	very ugly	非常醜
5	very beautiful	非常美麗
6	very handsome	非常帥氣
7	fatter	較胖的
8	thinner	較瘦的
9	happier	較開心的
10	uglier	較醜的
11	more beautiful	較美麗的
12	more handsome	較帥氣的
13	the fattest	最胖的
14	the thinnest	最瘦的
15	the happiest	最開心的
16	the most beautiful	最美麗的
17	Who is the best?	誰是最棒的？
18	meet	認識；遇見
19	my family	我的家人
20	dad	爸爸；父親
21	brother	兄弟
22	sister	姐妹

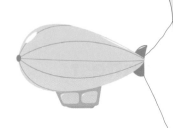

國家圖書館出版品預行編目資料

FUN 學美國各學科 Preschool 閱讀課本 . 2, 形容詞篇 (寂天隨身聽 APP 版)
/ Michael A. Putlack, e-Creative Contents 著 ; 歐寶妮譯 . -- 二版 . -- 臺北
市 : 寂天文化 , 2023.07
　　面 ; 　公分
ISBN 978-626-300-198-5 (菊 8K 平裝)

1.CST: 英語 2.CST: 形容詞

805.164　　　　　　　　　　　　　　　　112010251

FUN學 美國各學科
Preschool 閱讀課本 二版
Preschool 形容詞篇

作　者	Michael A. Putlack & e-Creative Contents
譯　者	歐寶妮
編　輯	林晨禾／歐寶妮
主　編	丁宥暄
內文排版	林書玉（課本）／謝青秀（練習本）
封面設計	林書玉
製程管理	洪巧玲
發 行 人	黃朝萍
出 版 者	寂天文化事業股份有限公司
電　話	02-2365-9739
傳　真	02-2365-9835
網　址	www.icosmos.com.tw
讀者服務	onlineservice@icosmos.com.tw
出版日期	2023 年 7 月　二版二刷 （寂天雲隨身聽 APP 版）

郵撥帳號　　1998620-0　　寂天文化事業股份有限公司

訂書金額未滿 1000 元，請外加運費 100 元。

〔若有破損，請寄回更換，謝謝〕